ReadZone Books Limited

50 Godfrey Avenue
Twickenham
TW2 7PF
UK

First published in this edition 2014

© in this edition ReadZone Books Limited 2014
© in text and illustrations Scoular Anderson 2007

Scoular Anderson has asserted his right under the Copyright Designs and Patents Act 1988 to be identified as the author and illustrator of this work.

Every attempt has been made by the Publisher to secure appropriate permissions for material reproduced in this book. If there has been any oversight we will be happy to rectify the situation in future editions or reprints. Written submissions should be made to the Publisher.

British Library Cataloguing in Publication Data (CIP) is available for this title.

Printed in Malta by Melita Press

ISBN 978 1 78322 206 3

Visit our website: www.readzonebooks.com

LOVELY, LOVELY PIRATE GOLD

by Scoular Anderson

READZ☼NE

When the pirate captain
opened his chest...

...looking for socks and an itchy vest...

...he found – a map!

He ran to his crew...

9

"You know what to do
with this wonderful clue –
it's time to hunt for treasure."

So they sailed away…

...to a wide, sandy bay...

...where they all
lent a hand...

14

...to dig in the sand.

15

The sand piled up as they dug for loot...

17

...but they found no treasure,
just a smelly old boot!

The captain cried, "It's just not fair!"
Then stamped his foot and pulled his hair.

The cabin boy looked at
the map…

...first like this, then like that.

23

At last he told them with
a frown,
"The treasure map was
upside down!"

They raced away to
dig again.

This time the captain did not complain!

29

Then each pirate wore a smile,
when each pirate had a pile
of lovely, lovely pirate gold.

Did you enjoy this book?

Look out for more *Magpies* titles –
fun stories in 150 words

The Clumsy Cow by Julia Moffat and Lisa Williams
ISBN 978 1 78322 157 8

The Disappearing Cheese by Paul Harrison and Ruth Rivers
ISBN 978 1 78322 470 8

Flying South by Alan Durant and Kath Lucas
ISBN 978 1 78322 410 4

Fred and Finn by Madeline Goodey and Mike Gordon
ISBN 978 1 78322 411 1

Growl! by Vivian French and Tim Archbold
ISBN 978 1 78322 412 8

I wish I was an Alien by Vivian French and Lisa Williams
ISBN 978 1 78322 413 5

Lovely, lovely Pirate Gold by Scoular Anderson
ISBN 978 1 78322 206 3

Pet to School Day by Hilary Robinson and Tim Archbold
ISBN 978 1 78322 471 5

Tall Tilly by Jillian Powell and Tim Archbold
ISBN 978 1 78322 414 2

Terry the Flying Turtle by Anna Wilson and Mike Gordon
ISBN 978 1 78322 415 9

Too Small by Kay Woodward and Deborah van de Leijgraaf
ISBN 978 1 78322 156 1

Turn off the Telly by Charlie Gardner and Barbara Nascimbeni
ISBN 978 1 78322 158 5